For
Freddie

This paperback edition first published in 2013 by Andersen Press Ltd.
First published in Great Britain in 2012 by Andersen Press Ltd.,
20 Vauxhall Bridge Road, London SW1V 2SA.
Published in Australia by Random House Australia Pty.,
Level 3, 100 Pacific Highway, North Sydney, NSW 2060.
Copyright © Jo Hodgkinson, 2012.
The rights of Jo Hodgkinson to be identified as the author and illustrator
of this work have been asserted by her in accordance
with the Copyright, Designs and Patents Act, 1988.
All rights reserved.
Colour separated in Switzerland by Photolitho AG, Zürich.
Printed and bound in Singapore by Tien Wah Press.

10 9 8 7 6 5 4 3 2 1

British Library Cataloguing in Publication Data available.

ISBN 978 1 84939 538 0

This book has been printed on acid-free paper

My Friend Nigel

ANDERSEN PRESS

JO HODGKINSON

Billy's dad and Billy's mum
Thought magic was a lot of fun.
You might think Bill would like it too
But quite the opposite was true.

Their spells were always going wrong
Mum's potions made a nasty pong.

While they liked magic quite a lot . . .

Billy
certainly
did not.

Bill peered at all their
strange supplies
Jellied bugs and pickled flies.
Bubbling potions,
lizard's scales,

And what was this?
A little snail?

"Oh, Mum, please no!
don't tell me he
Is for a magic recipe.

To do that would be so unkind
I have a better plan in mind.

Instead why don't you
say you'll let
Me keep this snail
as my new pet?"

Bill gave him Nigel
as a name,

He taught him how to play new games.

Said Dad to Mum, "Just give him time
He'll soon get bored of all that slime.

These spells will help us show our boy
Some other pets he could enjoy."

"We know you're
fond of your pet snail,

But have you thought about a Whale?

If not a whale, now let me see . . .
Perhaps a giant dancing bee!

This elephant does tricks you know
Unlike your snail who's rather slow.

This tiger here could be your guy
While Nigel is a little shy."

"I'm sorry but they'll have to go!
Oh Mum and Dad, why can't you see?
It's Nigel who's the pet for me."

But what Bill said,
he said too late
And Nigel didn't
hear his mate.

As Billy turned
to see his snail,
He saw instead
a slimy trail.

It read:

I think it's for the best,
I'm not as fun as all the rest.
I hope you find the perfect pet
And I'm so happy that we met.
I'm sorry that it had to end.
Lots of love from,
your old friend
XXX

As Billy shouted Nigel's name,
Dad's magic spells
went wrong again.
Things got crazy,
things went bad.

The tiger tried to eat Bill's dad.
The elephant was tickling mum.

The bee stung Billy on the bum.

As Nigel reached
to call the lift,
He heard Bill's cry
and being swift,

He pulled the skateboard
from his case

And WHIZZED along at lightning pace.

Then catapulted through the door,
And slid across the hallway floor.

But no one noticed Nigel Snail,
Or saw his super-slimy trail.

The tiger slipped onto his back

And knocked mum's potions off the rack.

And suddenly a puff of smoke
Made everybody cough and choke.

But as the smoke began to clear,
Those crazy beasts had disappeared.

Well Mum and Dad were pleased as punch
And made that snail a hero's lunch.

Mum gently patted
Nigel's shell
And said, "This snail
beats any spell
And now with magic
we are through.

We'll soon find something else to do.
You see at last we know it's true
A friendship can be magic too."

If you enjoyed this, you'll also love:

9781849390767

'This rollicking, rhythmical tale is a heart-warming treat!'
RED HOUSE CHILDREN'S BOOK AWARD

Chosen as one of World Book Day 2011's pre-school recommended picture books

Shortlisted for the Cambridgeshire Picture Book Award

Shortlisted for the Stockport Children's Book Award

Shortlisted for Booktrust's Early Years Award